# INSIDE

## THE MAZE RUNNER

# THE GUIDE TO THE GLADE

VERONICA DEETS

**Delacorte Press**

Text copyright © 2014 by Random House LLC

© 2014 Twentieth Century Fox Film Corporation. All rights reserved.

Book design by Georgia Rucker

All rights reserved. Published in the United States by Delacorte Press, an imprint of Random House Children's Books, a division of Random House LLC, a Penguin Random House Company, New York.

Delacorte Press is a registered trademark and the colophon is a trademark of Random House LLC.

Visit us on the Web! randomhouseteens.com

Educators and librarians, for a variety of teaching tools, visit us at RHTeachersLibrarians.com

Library of Congress Cataloging-in-Publication Data is available upon request.

ISBN 978-0-553-51108-6 (trade)
ISBN 978-0-553-51109-3 (ebook)

Printed in the United States of America

10 9 8 7 6 5 4 3 2 1

First Edition

# CONTENTS

# INTRODUCTION

# "WHAT IS THIS PLACE?"

**W**hen Thomas wakes up in the Box, he has no memories. It's the same for every boy who arrives in the Glade. Except for the supplies that arrive in the Box every month, and the puzzling letters *W.C.K.D.* stamped on those supplies, they have no clue who sent them to this strange place or why. They have no contact with the outside world. They know only one thing for certain: that there is no way out unless they solve the Maze that surrounds their new home. A Maze of ever-changing patterns, and filled with terrifying monsters. Is it a challenge, or is it a death sentence?

Enter the world of *The Maze Runner.* This is the guide to the Glade.

# THE
# RULES

"IF YOU WANT TO STAY HERE, I NEED TO KNOW THAT YOU CAN FOLLOW THE RULES, THAT YOU CAN LIVE AS PART OF A GROUP—A *FAMILY.*"

"FIRST, EVERYONE DOES THEIR PART NO ROOM FOR FREELOADERS."

"SECOND, DON'T EVER HURT ANOTHER GLADER. NONE OF THIS WORKS IF WE CAN'T TRUST EACH OTHER. BUT MOST IMPORTANTLY . . ."

# "NEVER GO OUTSIDE THE WALLS."

# THE BOX

"WHATEVER WE NEED
THE BOX PROVIDES. . . .
EVERYTHING ELSE IS
UP TO US."

Every Glader wakes up in darkness, to the deafening sound of screeching metal and the stomach-dropping lurch of being jerked skyward. This is the Box. The experience is terrifying.

Gradually, light begins to appear from above, and suddenly an alarm sounds over the whir of machinery. It grows louder and louder until the Box lurches to a stop. The doors are thrown open.

"DAY ONE,
GREENIE.
RISE AND
SHINE."

The Box is the entry point to the Glade. It's a large metal utility elevator. The Box is sent up once a month with supplies and a new boy. Not one boy has any memories of who he was or where he came from. His first name is the only information that will eventually return.

THE
GLADE

"WELCOME TO THE GLADE. WELCOME TO OUR HOME."

"THIS IS ALL WE'VE GOT. AND WE'VE WORKED HARD FOR IT. RESPECT THIS PLACE—FOLLOW THE RULES—AND YOU AND I ARE GONNA GET ALONG JUST FINE."

The Glade is a wide expanse of lush green land surrounded by towering stone walls. The Gladers have set up their home using the Glade's natural resources, and what has come up in the Box, to build the structures and raise the food they need to survive.

# THE LOOKOUT TREE

## "HOPE YOU'RE NOT AFRAID OF HEIGHTS."

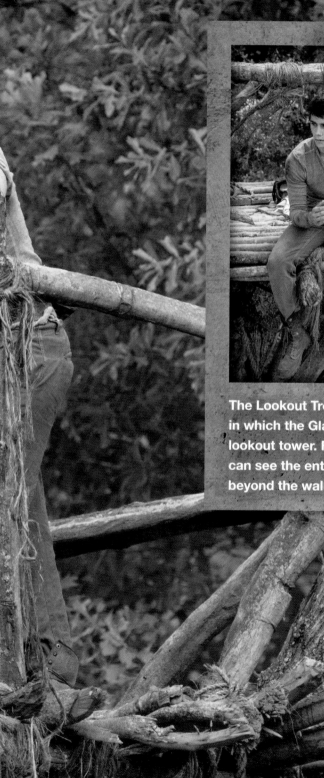

The Lookout Tree is a dead tree in which the Gladers have built a lookout tower. From the top, they can see the entire Glade and just beyond the walls of the Maze.

# THE
# HOMESTEAD

The Homestead is where the Gladers sleep. It's a thatched structure built out of branches from the woods. The Gladers sleep in hammocks strung up bunk-style both inside the building and outside in the open air.

# THE FOOD
# SHACK

The Food Shack is Frypan's domain. It's where all the food is stored, prepared, cooked, and served.

# THE
# FIELDS

The Fields are where the Gladers grow all their food.
The boys plant the seeds that arrive in the Box. They
tend the land, then harvest the crops. Newt is the
Keeper of the Fields.

# THE COUNCIL HALL

The Council Hall was built right up against a corner of the Maze wall. The Keepers run the Council, but everyone in the Glade has a voice. When the Gladers need to make an important decision, the Keepers call a meeting and all the Gladers meet in the Council Hall to vote.

There are some decisions that only the Keepers can make. For these, they hold a private Meeting of the Keepers in this building.

# THE MAP ROOM

Every day, when the Runners return from the Maze, they go directly to the Map Room to record the new patterns they've discovered on their run. Using this information, they've built a scale model of the Maze out of sticks collected from the woods. Every section, every passage, and every turn is mapped out in careful detail.

# THE PIT

A holding cell dug into the earth, the Pit has two main functions. It is generally where Greenies spend their first night in the Glade. Here, a Greenie can calm down in a solitary place after the shocking experience of arriving in the Glade in the Box. It's also a secure location to hold a Glader who might be dangerous, or a punishment for breaking a rule of the Glade.

# THE WALL

"MAKE YOUR MARK."

Every Glader carves his name in the Wall when he first arrives in the Glade. When a Glader dies, his name gets crossed off.

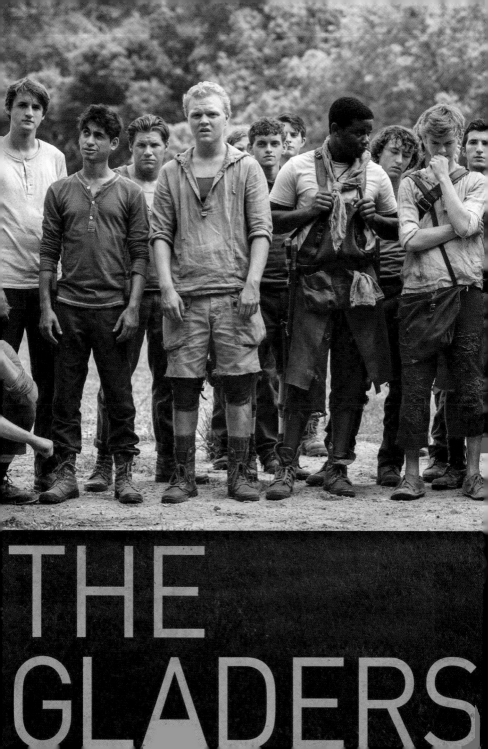

"THE MOST IMPORTANT THING WE HAVE IS EACH OTHER. WE'RE ALL IN THIS TOGETHER."

# ALBY

"SOMEONE
HAD TO BE
THE FIRST,
RIGHT?"

Alby is the Head Keeper of the Glade and leader of the Gladers. He was the first to arrive in the Glade, and the month he spent alone there turned him into the determined leader he is. Alby is calm and kind but also a stern peacekeeper.

# NEWT

"WE CAN'T
RISK LOSING
ANYONE ELSE,
THOMAS."

Newt was one of the first boys to arrive in the Glade after Alby. He's the Keeper of the Fields. Newt has a wry sense of humor, and he quickly becomes one of Thomas's biggest supporters and closest friends. Newt is brave and loyal to the end.

# CHUCK

"YOU CAN LOOK ALL YOU WANT, BUT YOU BETTER **NOT** GO OUT THERE."

Chuck is the youngest Glader and was the last to arrive in the Box before Thomas. Because he was the last Greenie, he is assigned to be Thomas's guide. Chuck is open-hearted and earnest, and he connects instantly with Thomas and looks up to him. He is the closest thing Thomas has to a little brother.

# MINHO

"BE ALERT, FOLLOW MY LEAD, AND NEVER FORGET THE NUMBER ONE RULE: NEVER STOP RUNNING."

Minho is Keeper of the Runners. He's fast and strong, but he's also enigmatic and thoughtful and tends to hang around the edges of the group. Whatever he's seen while running in the Maze has made him who he is. Minho becomes a close confidant of Thomas and his right-hand man in the effort to solve the Maze.

# GALLY

"EVERYTHING
STARTED
GOING WRONG
THE MINUTE
YOU SHOWED UP."

Gally was one of the first Gladers and is one of the oldest boys in the Glade. He's the Keeper of the Builders. He's also an opinionated member of the Council of the Keepers. He is deeply suspicious of Thomas and marks his arrival as the point when everything started to change. Gally is determined to save his home, the Glade, from harm. He's strong and willful and has the tendency to lash out with fists rather than turn the other cheek.

# BEN

"HE BELONGS
TO THE MAZE
NOW."

Ben is Minho's partner in the Maze. He's one of the fastest Runners and one of the only Gladers who can keep pace with the Keeper. Ben's fate is marked when he's stung by a Griever and goes through the Changing.

# FRYPAN

"DINNER IS
SERVED, BOYS."

Frypan is responsible for cooking for all the Gladers. One of the first to arrive in the Glade, he's also one of the oldest boys. Frypan belongs to the Council of Keepers as the Keeper of the Cooks. He is fiercely proud of his work and dedicated to his job. The other Gladers may subject him to good-natured ribbing about his cooking, but his food is excellent.

# WINSTON

"MINHO TRUSTS YOU. THAT'S GOOD ENOUGH FOR ME."

Winston is the Keeper of the Slicers.
He's good with his knives and with the
livestock. Winston's brave enough to face
a Griever if it means escaping the Maze.

# JEFF

## "HOW LONG DO YOU THINK WE CAN LAST?"

Jeff is a Med-jack and takes his job seriously. Even though he arrived in the Glade with no memories, he took naturally to first aid and does his best to help injured Gladers—who were usually Slicers, before Thomas came.

# THOMAS

"I THINK IT'S TIME TO FIND OUT WHAT WE'RE REALLY UP AGAINST."

From the moment Thomas arrives in the Glade, it's clear he's different from the others. Thomas is curious, and unlike the other boys, who are afraid of the Maze, he's drawn to it. Thomas is a born leader. He is charismatic and kind, and won't accept the strange situation he's found himself in. He wants out.

# THE MAZE

"NO ONE
SURVIVES
A NIGHT IN
THE MAZE."

The Glade sits at the center of the Maze. The Maze is built of enormous stone walls that stretch at least a hundred feet into the sky, covered in thick patches of ivy. None of the Gladers know who built it, how, or why.

"WE'RE TRAPPED HERE, AREN'T WE?"

# THE MAZE
# DOORS AND
# WALLS

"TRUST ME. IF THERE WAS A WAY OUT, WE WOULD HAVE FOUND IT BY NOW."

There is one passage into and out of the Maze. The Maze doors open every morning and close every night like clockwork. When the doors are open during daylight hours, the Runners run the Maze. They map it and memorize it, looking for a way out. But every night, after the doors close, the Maze walls shift into a new pattern. The Runners have figured out that some sections remain in place, and they use these to guide their missions.

# AREAS TO KNOW IN THE MAZE

**THE BLADES:** a labyrinth of monolithic metal slabs that resembles a forest.

**THE NARROWS:** a network of narrow corridors in the Maze.

**THE INNER RING:** a stark contrast to the Narrows, the ring is composed of open spaces and cavernous courtyards.

# THE RUNNERS

"*NO ONE* WANTS TO BE A RUNNER. BESIDES, YOU HAVE TO BE CHOSEN."

The Runners are the only Gladers who know what's out there in the Maze. They are the strongest and fastest Gladers. If the Runners don't make it back before the doors close, they're stuck in the Maze overnight. As long as there has been a Maze and there have been Gladers, no one has ever lived through a night on the other side of the Maze doors.

# THE GRIEVERS

"THAT, MY FRIEND, WAS A GRIEVER. NOT TO WORRY. YOU'RE SAFE IN HERE WITH US. NOTHING GETS THROUGH THOSE WALLS."

Monstrous creatures that are part nature and part science, Grievers roam the Maze at night. Grievers are the reason the Gladers are terrified of being left in the Maze when the doors close. No one has ever survived an encounter with a Griever.

# THE GIRL

"SHE'S THE
LAST ONE.
EVER."

After Thomas arrives in the Glade, the Box comes up again, earlier than usual. In it the Gladers find the strangest cargo ever: a girl. She arrives unconscious, clutching a mysterious note in her hand. Most disturbing is that she recognizes Thomas.

The Girl is Teresa. She's the only girl to ever arrive in the Glade, yet Thomas has dreamed of her before. In his dreams she tells him, "Everything is going to change."

Equally strange is that Teresa knows Thomas. She remembers pieces of her life before the Box and the Glade. Teresa arrives in the Glade with more than just a note— two syringes are in her pocket.

Thomas and Teresa are different from the other Gladers. But do they hold the key to solving the Maze, or were they sent to the Glade for darker reasons?

With Teresa's arrival, everything the Gladers have ever known changes.

REMEMBER . . .
W.C.K.D. IS GOOD.